By the Tree

Written by Marilyn Minkoff
Illustrated by Mark Schroder

"Look! A ball is by the tree!" said Will.

"Give it to me!" said Manny.
"Give it to me!"

"No!" said Will.

"Then I'll run and tell my mom," said Manny.

"Look! A bat is by the tree!"
said Manny.

"Give it to me!" said Will.
"Give it to me!"

"No!" said Manny.

"Then I'll run and tell my mom," said Will.

"I will not give it to you," said Manny.
"But we can share."